The Summer of the Pike

The summer of the pike

Jutta Richter

Illustrated by Quint Buchholz

Translated from the German
by Anna Brailovsky

MILKWEED EDITIONS

© Carl Hanser Verlag München Wien 2004
© 2004, Interior art by Quint Buchholz.

Published 2006 by Milkweed Editions
Printed in Canada
Cover design by Percolator
Cover illustration of fish by
    Michael C. Newell
Author photo by Brigitte Friedrich
Interior design by Percolator
Interior illustrations by Quint Buchholz
The text of this book is set in FF Celeste.
06 07 08 09 10   5 4 3 2 1
First Edition

Milkweed Editions, a nonprofit publisher, gratefully acknowledges sustaining support from Emilie and Henry Buchwald; Bush Foundation; Patrick and Aimee Butler Family Foundation; Cargill Value Investment; Timothy and Tara Clark Family Charitable Fund; Dougherty Family Foundation; Ecolab Foundation; General Mills Foundation; John and Joanne Gordon; Greystone Foundation; Institute for Scholarship in the Liberal Arts, College of Arts and Sciences, University of Notre Dame; Constance B. Kunin; Marshall BankFirst; Marshall Field's Gives; May Department Stores Company Foundation; McKnight Foundation; a grant from the Minnesota State Arts Board, through an appropriation by the Minnesota State Legislature, a grant from the National Endowment for the Arts, and private funders; an award from the National Endowment for the Arts, which believes that a great nation deserves great art; Navarre Corporation; Debbie Reynolds; St. Paul Travelers Foundation; Ellen and Sheldon Sturgis; Target Foundation; Gertrude

Sexton Thompson Charitable Trust (George R. A. Johnson, Trustee); James R. Thorpe Foundation; Toro Foundation; Serene and Christopher Warren; W. M. Foundation; and Xcel Energy Foundation.

Library of Congress
Cataloging-in-Publication Data

Richter, Jutta, 1955-
    [Hechtsommer. English]
    The summer of the pike / Jutta Richter; translated by Anna Brailovsky; illustrations by Quint Buchholz.—1st ed.
        p.   cm.
Summary: Three children who live on the grounds of a German castle spend the summer trying to catch a pike trapped in the moat, while the mother of two of the children is slowly dying of cancer.
    ISBN-13: 978-1-57131-671-4
(hardcover: alk. paper)
    ISBN-10: 1-57131-671-X
(hardcover: alk. paper)
    ISBN-13: 978-1-57131-672-1
(pbk.: alk. paper)
    ISBN-10: 1-57131-672-8
(pbk.: alk. paper)
    [1. Cancer—Fiction. 2. Fishing—Fiction. 3. Mothers—Fiction.
4. Germany—Fiction.] I. Brailovsky, Anna. II. Buchholz, Quint, ill. III. Title.
    PZ7.R41544 Su
    [Fic]–dc22
                                2006012645

The Summer of the Pike

IT WAS ONE OF THOSE SUMMERS that goes on forever. And no one would have believed, back then, that it would be our last. We simply couldn't believe that. Just like we couldn't imagine that it would ever be winter again—a bitter, cold winter with real snow and a thick layer of ice over the moat.

It was one of those summers that goes on forever. It began in May. The sun shone every day. The peonies put forth buds, the catkins on the chestnut trees exploded overnight. The mustard field was aglow with yellow flowers. And high above us the swallows sliced through the deep, endless sky.

Only the water still kept its winter color: black and impenetrable. But if we stretched over the parapet of the stone bridge long enough, we could make out the little redeye fish sunning themselves just under the water's surface.

"Bug-eyed," I said. "If you stare for a long time, you'll go bug-eyed."

"Yeah," said Daniel. "And then you can see all the way down to the bottom, and there's the pike!"

Lucas was very excited and when he spoke his voice

grew high and loud. "Yeah, sure! And when we can see the pike, all we need is a fishing line and a pike hook."

"Knucklehead," said Daniel. "You need a bait trap and a hand net, too!"

"What for?"

"The trap for the baitfish, and the net to get the pike out. He'll tear your line clear through if you try to pull him out."

"And what's the baitfish for?" asked Lucas.

"To lure him in," said Daniel, and spit into the water.

Curious, the little redeye swam closer. Then they suddenly scattered and were gone.

"There he is!" Lucas cried.

And for a tenth of a second, right under the surface, I really did glimpse the silver belly of the pike, before it shot back down again into the black, impenetrable depths.

Above us fluttered a cawing flock of magpies, and two coots drifted by under the bridge, jerking their heads. The sun warmed our backs, and when the water was calm and smooth again, Daniel said:

"We're gonna get him! If you've got bug-eyes, you can catch pike, too!"

Fishing was not allowed. There were signs posted on the trees near the bank: *No fishing. Violators will be prosecuted by the owner.*

"Oh, he won't even notice!" Daniel said.

"But what if the earl comes by? Or the caretaker? Or anyone at all?" asked Lucas.

"Man, then we're just sitting on the bridge! The fishing line's see-through. The spool fits in your hand! Make a fist, you're all set!"

"And what about Mom? Mom doesn't want us fishing either!" Lucas said.

Daniel only stared into the black water and said nothing more.

An air-gun shot rang out near the caretaker's house and the magpies flew over the red tile roof, complaining loudly.

Lucas drew closer to me.

"Did you know that the gimpy hen has four chicks now?" he asked softly. "They just hatched the day before yesterday. Daniel hasn't seen them yet, but I have! And Mom said she would come, too, and then she'll catch one for me and I can hold it . . . D'you want me to show you guys the chicks?"

I nodded.

"C'mon, old man! Your brother's gonna show us the gimpy hen's chicks!"

Daniel didn't budge.

"I don't wanna go check out the chicks," he muttered. "I want the pike! Chicks are for babies!"

"Chicks are for babies!" Lucas aped. "My doofus brother doesn't want to!"

The peahen had only one foot. That was the nasty memento left over from last summer.

And every time the peahen limped across the yard,

I remembered what had happened and was ashamed of myself.

Because it was my fault that the hen only had one foot now. After all, I was the oldest.

Gisela had had to go to the hospital and I'd promised to look after things. Not just help out with homework for an hour like I usually did. No, really look after things, so that Daniel and Lucas wouldn't be alone in the afternoon until Peter came home. The afternoons were long and we whiled away the time fishing for redeye until evening came.

The dumb little redeye could be lured with bread. They liked white bread best of all, really fresh white bread. And there was always plenty of it in the bread box in Gisela's kitchen.

That's because every evening Peter brought a fresh loaf of white bread home in his briefcase. Gisela told him to, before she had to leave.

"And don't forget to always bring a loaf of bread for the boys! They're hungry after school! And remember, they like white bread best! Don't forget!"

Peter probably would have been pretty mad if he'd known that we fed half of his white bread to the stupid redeye, but he didn't have a clue. On the contrary, he was always happy in the evenings to see that not a crumb was left.

I'd hidden a smirk and thought how dumb fathers really were if they didn't even know that two boys could never in their lives eat a whole big loaf of white bread by themselves.

———

But catching the redeye turned out not to be as easy as I thought. The thing with the bucket didn't work.

We'd tied the bucket to Gisela's green laundry line and lowered it just under the water's surface. Then we threw pieces of bread into the water. The water bubbled up whenever the redeye snapped greedily at the bread, and then we pulled the bucket up. But we were too slow every time. The redeye scattered and the bucket remained empty.

"This fishing's for amateurs," grumbled Daniel. "You won't catch any redeye this way in a hundred years! Only a broad could think that up!"

He spit a gob into the water.

"You have a better idea, maybe?"

"I have!" Daniel said. He rummaged in his pants pocket and put a roll of nylon line on the wall. From the other pocket, he pulled out a small fishhook with a sharp point. He began to thread the transparent line into the eye of the hook. Then he wrapped the end around the line five times and pulled it tight.

"Where'd you get the hook?" I asked.

"Traded it!" answered Daniel and stuck a pellet of white bread on the hook.

"But that's fishing, and we're not allowed!" said Lucas.

Daniel slid the line into the water.

"And what if someone catches us?" Lucas asked.

I put my arm around him and we peered into the water.

The smallest redeye immediately swam closer and

began nibbling at the bread. Suddenly, a large one came shooting in between them and greedily swallowed the whole clump. Daniel gave it a bit of line before pulling it in with a sharp tug. The line went taut and we saw the redeye trying to dive under. It flapped its tail, it pulled and tugged, but it was caught firmly on the hook.

A fish on the line, I thought. Like a dog.

"Pull it up," cried Lucas.

And Daniel pulled. The redeye wriggled like mad, doubled up and flapped its tail.

Lucas grabbed hold of it, but it slipped through his fingers and then hung in the air until he grabbed it again, and this time he held on tight.

"What now?" he asked.

"Now we have to take the hook out," said Daniel.

"Then do it, but make it quick!"

"I'm not touching that," said Daniel.

"Chicken!"

Lucas pried open the fish's mouth with his thumb and forefinger. The hook had buried itself firmly up in front. Lucas took hold of the hook and pushed it in a little deeper. We heard a faint crack as it came loose. The redeye didn't wriggle anymore. It looked pretty dead.

"It's a goner," I said. "Throw it back in!"

For a second, the redeye lay motionless in the water, then it suddenly flapped its tail and dove down into the blackness.

Lucas's hand was covered in slime and reeked of fish. He wiped it off on his pants.

"When they're stressed, they always get slimy," said Daniel.

That's how fish break out in a cold sweat, I thought. Being slippery is their only chance. When they make themselves slippery, they can even slip out of the heron's beak. But somehow it was kind of gross, too, and I didn't really feel like fishing anymore.

"We should do something else," I suggested. "How about throwing some darts?"

"You've gotta be kidding," said Lucas. "We finally get the hang of this fishing thing and now you don't feel like it anymore."

"I just don't think it's good," I said. "The hook must hurt the fish for sure. Really, it's cruelty to animals!"

"Bull," said Daniel. "You just saw how alive it was, didn't you? By now it doesn't even know that it swallowed the hook. Fish don't have any memory."

Or any voice, I thought. Fish can't even scream.

Daniel tried to roll up the nylon line again, but it was so tangled he couldn't. He cursed softly. Then he took out his hunting knife and simply cut the tangled piece out.

By the time Gisela came home from the hospital, the manor courtyard was littered with transparent bits of nylon line. For we'd been fishing every afternoon, and even I had been seized by this strange fever. A tingling in the belly whenever we made the bread-covered hook dance in the water and the stupid redeye pounced on it. Would they bite? Or would they just nibble off the clump of bread like they so often did?

And that's when the thing with the peahen happened.

For as long as I can remember, the pair of peacocks had lived on the manor grounds. We called the male Pauly, and even in the winter, if I opened the window, I could call him from the roof. Then he'd take off and fly ponderously over the moat because he knew I would throw him some corn kernels. The hen was shy and always came a bit later. And she wouldn't eat out of our hands, either.

In the summer, the peacocks slept in the old chestnut tree at night and pierced the stillness with their cries whenever they were wakened by a noise—laughter, or singing, or a cough, or the footsteps of couples strolling in the moonlight.

Lucas saw it first. He was waiting for me by the door when I came home from school.

"The hen is sick," he said. "She's limping and her foot is all black. Come with me, you have to see it for yourself!"

We ran to the south lawn, where the peacocks hunted for worms in the daytime. I took along a handful of corn. We called Pauly, and Pauly came, and behind him, hesitant and distrustful, came the peahen. When she was close enough, I saw what had happened.

The thin, transparent fishing line had wound itself tight around her leg. Her foot had turned completely black and the toes dangled limp and lifeless below. She had pulled her injured foot up and hopped on the other foot.

Lucas held my hand really tight.

"That's our fishing line," he whispered. "We have to do something!"

For three days, we tried all afternoon to catch the hen. With nets and blankets and bits of bread and kernels of corn. But the hen was faster than us. Over and over, she flapped her wings and flew, screeching loudly, over the moat. And on the third afternoon, the caretaker caught us at it.

He stood suddenly before us, as if he'd sprung up from the ground. With his heavy hunting boots and his green knee britches, hands planted firmly on his hips, he glared down at us in fish-eyed fury and began to bellow. What on earth did we think we were doing! We must be completely out of our minds! How dare we hunt the earl's peacocks! And we could bet on it that, next time, our parents would have notice, in writing, that we were never to be allowed to set foot on the south lawn again!

He didn't even notice that the hen had a lame leg. And we didn't have the nerve to tell him, because then the whole thing with the fishing would come out, and because we were afraid of him.

When he was gone, Daniel threw himself down on the lawn and cried. I had never seen him cry like that before. His shoulders shook and he sobbed loudly into the grass.

"That's my fishing line! It's my fault! It's my fault if she dies!"

"No, no," I said. "It was an accident! You can't do anything about it!"

"Can too!" sobbed Daniel as he sprang up. "It's always my fault!" he cried, and ran off.

"D'you think she's really going to die?" asked Lucas,

taking my hand.

I didn't know. I only knew that a shadow had fallen over that summer and I would not forget it.

We didn't fish anymore. And by the time fall came, the peahen had become the gimpy hen. Her black toes had fallen off, but she still lived.

AND NOW SHE HAD FOUR CHICKS. And Daniel didn't want to see them and was angry.

"You can forget about Mom, anyway. She never keeps her promises!"

"She does too!" said Lucas.

"Does not!" Daniel kicked the wall. "Does not! Does not! Does not!"

I had a vague inkling of what he meant, and I also knew that something was not the same as it was before. But nobody would explain it to us. They'd only say that Gisela had to take it easy, that she had this stupid thing, that the doctors would take care of it all right.

If we asked questions, the grown-ups would shrug their shoulders and say, it'll be okay.

But they said it with an undertone and then quickly asked how school was and were we studying hard.

Gisela had not gone to work since the beginning of May, even though all she had to do was walk thirty steps across the courtyard to the caretaker's office. Thirty steps that she had walked every morning for as long as we could remember. She had waved to us from the office window when we came home from kindergarten at noon, had waved to us when we played in the sandbox in the afternoons, had waved to us on foggy November days when our botched math homework made us stomp in the puddles.

Thirty steps, for as long as we could remember, and she ran breathless and hurried and took really long steps, as though she'd otherwise be too late: late for the office, late coming home, late to go running, for the PTA, for the birthday party. She was always on her way somewhere, she never had time.

And I can hear her voice calling Daniel: "Daniel, come inside already! And bring your brother!"

And then I hear her chew them out because the two of them smell like fish again. "When are you going to put an end to this, huh? What do you always have to go grabbing those fish for? Go wash your hands right now! And I mean thoroughly!"

"She's got certified sick leave," said my mother. "It'll be okay, don't worry your little head about it."

But our heads were worried.

In the afternoons, we sat in our climbing tree and wondered why it was called certified sick leave. We took long pauses between speaking and in the pauses, I counted the flecks of sunlight glinting through the leafy canopy.

It wasn't fair that Gisela was certified sick, and Daniel said: "If I could, I'd certify Mom well."

"And then everything would be like before," said

Lucas. "And Mom wouldn't have to lie in bed all the time, and she'd be chewing us out again, too!"

Daniel tore off a branch and began to whip the tree trunk. Torn bits of leaf flew about our heads.

"Cut it out!" I said.

But Daniel didn't cut it out.

"Cer-ti-fied-sick!" he laughed, and whipped along to the beat. "Cer-ti-fied-sick! Cer-ti-fied-sick!" And the tears ran down his cheeks and I didn't know if he was laughing or crying.

On the eighth of May, the mustard flower buds burst open. In the morning, on our way to school, everything was just the way it had always been: the light fog over the moat, the heron on his hunting perch, the beech tree blood red in the early sunlight, and all around the dull green of the mustard field.

The school bus stood in front of the elementary school.

"See you in the afternoon," called Lucas and ran across the schoolyard.

Daniel and I climbed on the bus.

We could have gone later, but Gisela didn't want us to.

"You're going together! And that's that! One for all and all for one!"

And actually, it was better that way, because the second bus was always much too full and too loud.

Daniel didn't speak. Mornings, he was real pale and

real tired. He sat next to me, gazing out the window and smelling of sleep. I knew that he was still dreaming and that I had to let him be.

The bus drove through the farmsteads, past hedged earthworks and pastures and horse enclosures. Sometimes we saw deer feeding in the fields.

The farms were large and lay scattered far apart, and the farm kids who lived there had hyphenated names: Schulze-Horn and Schulze-Wettering and Schulze-Eschenbach, and even their first names were not like ours: Marie-Therese Schulze-Horn, Anna-Sofia Schulze-Wettering, Hubert Schulze-Eschenbach . . .

The farm kids were almost always fighting with the village kids, but they didn't bother us. After all, we were the kids from the manor.

"Manor children are special," Gisela had said.

"Keep that in mind and behave yourselves! If you're invited over, you take just one piece of cake and ask what you can do to help. Mind you, remember that!" She'd given Daniel a little smack and added: "And you! Don't just stand there all stiff the whole time! Follow your brother's example! You have to be friendly and say hello politely when you come into a house!"

"Oh, don't be so strict all the time," my mother had said and put her arm around Daniel. "He's just a little shy, he'll grow out of it!"

Daniel had turned red and I'd been embarrassed for my mother. Daniel wasn't shy. He just didn't talk a lot, but when he said something, it was important.

Grown-ups always acted as if they knew us so perfectly well. But in fact they didn't have a clue.

The farm kids didn't play with us because we were manor kids, and the village kids didn't like us because the farm kids left us alone. But we didn't tell anyone, least of all the grown-ups. They wouldn't have understood anyway. It was just the three of us, and that was enough.

The school bus was getting fuller and fuller. We sat in our usual seats right behind the driver and Daniel gazed out the window and daydreamed. Just past the Schulze-Wettering farmyard, there was a dead cat by the side of the road. Daniel gave me a nudge.

"Didja see that?"

I nodded.

"If that was my cat, I'd be bawling! But her—she's laughing!" He nodded in Anna-Sofia's direction. And in fact, Anna-Sofia Schulze-Wetterling and Marie-Therese had put their heads together and were giggling.

"Maybe it wasn't hers," I said.

"Wanna bet?"

Daniel turned his head away and stared out the window.

I knew he was furious, because there was nothing in the world he wanted more than a cat. But Peter remained obstinate. "That's enough now. Your mother can't tolerate cat hair. As long as your mother is ill, I won't have any animals in this house! Much less any cats!"

Past the Schulze-Eschenbach farm, Daniel suddenly said: "She's going bald."

"Who's going bald?"

"My mom."

I flinched. "You're nuts!"

"I've seen it. She runs a hand through her hair and the hair comes out!"

Gisela's hair—that was some hair she had, just like Snow White, long and dark.

Before, she'd always put it in a braid that bounced on her back when she ran across the courtyard. Now she usually wore a head scarf, and I'd figured she thought it looked nice. Mothers are often trying new stuff out. My mother's hair had been red the last four weeks, fire-engine red. She looked like Raggedy Ann. I'd never go about looking like that, but there you have it.

"I don't believe it!" I said. "You're just imagining it. And cut it out please!"

"I've seen it!" said Daniel softly, and then he didn't say anything more.

When we came back from school that afternoon, the mustard flower buds had burst open. We could see the field glowing with them from far away.

For us, those were the most beautiful colors in the world: the yellow of the mustard, the blood red of the beech, and above, the deep blue of the sky.

"It makes you happy just to look at it!" Lucas had said once. And it was true.

But today it was different, for I had to think of Gisela's hair, and I was scared.

———

My mother was standing in the kitchen, ironing.

"How was school?"

"Great!"

My mother laughed. We'd been playing this game for years. Every afternoon, the same question. Every afternoon, the same answer.

We called it the how-was-school-great game. My mother had told me that my grandmother used to ask that question every afternoon too. "As a kid, I hated it," she had said.

"So why do you ask?"

"Because I'm your mother and that's what mothers ask!"

She ironed and she laughed and her fiery red hair glowed in the sun.

"Mom? Is Gisela going bald?"

I saw that she was startled. She set the iron aside.

"Who told you that?"

"Daniel!"

My mother sat down on the kitchen bench.

"Come over here, sweetie!"

I sat down next to her. She took a cigarette out of the pack, lit it, and blew the smoke out her nose. I waited for her to say something, but she just made a serious face and hurriedly went on smoking.

It was so quiet that I could hear the ticking of the clock in the living room. A fly buzzed at the window and from time to time the iron hissed out a little spurt of steam.

My mother cleared her throat.

"All right then," she said. "I'm going to explain it to you, but you have to promise not to tell Daniel. Much less Lucas."

I swallowed hard and nodded. I could hear my heart beating.

"Gisela has cancer," my mother said softly. "That's a horrible sickness, sweetie. And the doctors are trying to get the sickness out of Gisela's body with poison. The poison is so strong that it makes your hair fall out. The poison is so strong that Gisela feels nauseous. Then she has to throw up and go to bed."

"But will she get better, Mommy?"

I saw tears well up in my mother's eyes.

"I hope so," she said. "And Gisela hopes so. And the doctors hope so, too. Lots of people who've had it have gotten better again. And their hair," said my mother, "then their hair grows back. But you must promise me not to tell the boys. Gisela doesn't want that, and Peter doesn't either! Do you understand?"

I nodded again.

There's a Before and there's an After and there's a Now.

Now was the kitchen and the hissing iron and my mother, smoking with tears in her eyes, and the streaks of light that fell through the window onto the kitchen table. Now was the moment in which I wished I'd never asked.

Don't be so nosy. Children mustn't know about those

things. That's none of your business. You'll find out soon
enough!

Now was the moment in which I wanted to be a little
kid again. To fall asleep in my mother's lap. Or to make a
bed across two chairs in my grandmother's kitchen. The
grown-ups sit around the table and tell stories about long
ago. The do-you-remember-when stories. How fat Uncle
Ewald stole the little golden violin off the Christmas tree
and on Christmas morning, there was nothing but straw
in his stocking. Nothing but straw!

And fat Uncle Ewald, with his cigar, he laughs about
it, as if there's nothing funnier than a stocking full of
straw on Christmas morning. And I lie in my bed across
two chairs and the murmur of their stories lulls me into
sleep.

"Lots of people who've had it have gotten better again!"
my mother said.

But I knew that was a lie. Everyone who had cancer
died. My grandmother died, and fat Uncle Ewald with his
cigar, and even my first guinea pig . . . no one had ever
gotten well again after the word "cancer" was spoken.

Clearly, I thought, guinea pigs can't be expected to live
forever. But it's really not asking too much for mothers to
hold off dying at least until their kids are grown.

And I was confused and scared, and I would have

loved to slap that cigarette out of my mother's hand. After all, it said right there on the package: smoking causes cancer. But maybe that was a lie, too, because Gisela never did smoke.

On the eighth of May, the mustard flower buds burst open. In the morning, on our way to school, everything had been just the way it had always been, and now Gisela had cancer.

THE PIKE HOOK HAD THREE SHARP POINTS and was four times as big as the redeye hook. Daniel carefully unwrapped it from his handkerchief and put it down on the stone parapet of the bridge.

"You're not serious!" I said.

"And how!"

"And the net? And the baitfish trap?"

"Be here next week!"

"Where from?"

"Your mother promised. She's gonna drive me to the tackle shop!"

"I don't believe it!"

"Ask her yerself!"

I ran to the house and yanked the door open. My mother was lying on the couch taking her afternoon nap. I gave her a shake.

"Good grief, what is it now?"

"You're not going to do that!" I panted. "You can't possibly do that!"

"What can't I do?" my mother asked with annoyance.

"Drive Daniel to the tackle shop! You can't do that! He's only going to get a net and a trap, you know!"

"So? Why shouldn't he get them? He did save up for them, after all! If you saved your money, you could buy something too!"

"But that's not the point!" I shouted. "You have totally no clue!"

"Drop that tone, if you please!" My mother's voice grew dangerously quiet. It became a toneless whisper, like the hissing of a snake. She spoke very clearly and I knew how angry she was. But just then, I didn't care.

"But he only wants—" I shouted. My mother cut me off midsentence with a wave of her hand.

"Get out of here!" she whispered. "And shame on you! Shame on you for your envy!"

In my room, I threw myself down on my bed. And that's when I began to cry. I wasn't envious. I just didn't want Daniel to catch the pike.

If he had a net, he would pull him out. And when he pulled him out, he would finish him off. Just beat him to death. And I didn't want that!

While Daniel and Lucas fished for redeye, I sat in the climbing tree and fumed. Fumed about Daniel, fumed about my mother, and fumed about the whole world. And for the first time in my life, I wished I had a girlfriend. A girlfriend like Anna-Sofia Schulze-Wettering, that I could giggle, and whisper, and hang out with. A girlfriend I could lie around in the hay and talk about everything with. About Gisela, and the thing with the pike, and that people who have cancer always die.

A girl like Anna-Sofia Schulze-Wettering—she knew all about life, about being born and dying; she'd seen it a hundred times, when the calves came into this world and the swine were slaughtered. A girl like Anna-Sofia Schulze-Wettering—she'd certainly know the answers to my questions and not start bawling straightaway. After all, she hadn't cried about her dead cat.

From the climbing tree, I had a good view of the courtyard. I saw Peter coming home. He had his briefcase under his arm and he shuffled his feet as he walked, just like Daniel.

"He's going to trip over his own feet someday!" Gisela had always said to my mother when we were younger, and then Daniel would be on the verge of tears and she'd laugh and call him Daniela, and draw the "a" out for a real long time.

Peter pulled the house key from his jacket pocket and unlocked the door. As it opened, I saw Gisela for a single moment. She stood in the hall and gave Peter a hug, and I could see that she really didn't have any hair left.

I climbed down from the tree and got my bike out of the shed.

Before, we often went on bike rides in the afternoon. Gisela and my mother and Daniel and I. Lucas sat behind Gisela in the child seat because he couldn't ride a bike yet, but Daniel and I could ride, even with no hands, and fast, faster than the others. I knew every pothole along the forest path. I knew exactly when to brake to get around the barriers.

"She rides like a boy!" Gisela had said, and my mother had laughed and nodded and then the two of them sang, Gisela and my mother, loudly and in two-part harmony: "We All Live in a Yellow Submarine," and "Killing Me Softly with His Song," and "Long, Long Ago."

And Daniel had furtively rolled his eyes and made faces and pretended to gag, because he found it so embarrassing.

Just before the Schulze-Wettering farm, I lost my courage. I had pedaled like mad and imagined what I was going to say. I would ring the bell, and when Mrs. Schulze-Wettering opened the door, I would ask if Anna-Sofia was home. And Mrs. Schulze-Wettering would laugh and say: "Come on in. Won't Anna-Sofia be pleased!"

But maybe it wouldn't be like that at all. Maybe the guard dog would lunge at me, and Anna-Sofia's big brother would come out of the barn and yell: "Get lost! You're the one from the manor! Get off our farm!"

And actually, I didn't even know what I should say to Anna-Sofia. We'd never spoken to each other before and I couldn't very well just say: "Anna-Sofia Schulze-Wettering, will you be my friend?"

When I rode back over our bridge, Daniel and Lucas were still fishing. Lucas ran toward me. His eyes shone with excitement.

"Look at what we caught!"

Next to Daniel stood Gisela's green bucket, half full of water, and the water bubbled as if it were boiling. I counted seventeen redeye.

"I took every last one off the hook myself!" laughed Lucas. "My brother is too chicken. It grosses him out when they get slimy! He wouldn't have a single redeye if it wasn't for me!"

He reached out toward me, but I drew back: "Don't you touch me with your stinky fish fingers! I think you're both just revolting!"

Lucas stared at me, bewildered. The light in his eyes was gone. He hung his head.

"And besides, you're not even allowed to fish!" I said. "And I'm telling the caretaker!"

Daniel slowly pulled the hook out of the water, then turned around and put his arm around Lucas.

"Leave my brother alone!" he said softly. "And you can tell the caretaker all you want. For your information, we are too allowed to fish. Since yesterday. The earl came to see Mom and gave us permission!"

I was furious, shoved my bicycle into the shed and went into the house.

———

They sat around our kitchen table, and for one brief moment, I thought everything was just like before.

My mother was laughing, Peter grinned, and Gisela stirred sugar in her tea.

That's how they often used to sit together, in the early summer evenings, after Peter came home from work. They would tell stories, drink spiked fruit punch or dark beer, and sometimes they'd even let us try some. "But just a little sip, or else you'll get plastered!" But of course we hadn't believed them, because the punch tasted like Kool-Aid.

My mother laughed, Peter grinned, and Gisela stirred sugar in her tea. I remained standing in the kitchen doorway. "Well, come on over here, baby! Let me give you a hug!" said Gisela. "I haven't seen you up close in a long time!"

Her head scarf was dark red with little black dots and she'd wound it around like a turban. I wanted to ask her to show me how to tie a turban like that, but I didn't dare. Nor did I dare go to her and give her a hug. And so I just stood there and everyone stared at me and my mother said: "Well, don't just stand there all stiff!"

"Whatever is the matter with you?" asked Gisela. "You're not usually so shy."

I would have liked nothing better than to turn invisible, but instead I just turned red and hoped they wouldn't notice. But of course they did notice, and my mother laughed nervously and hastily said that it was puberty and I'd been acting standoffish for a long while now.

"Children grow up," said my mother, but Gisela just gave her a funny look and didn't believe a word of it.

"We had a falling-out," I mumbled.

Gisela gave a start.

"Why," asked Peter?

"Because they're always fishing and I think it's disgusting!"

Gisela began to cough. She kept on coughing until Peter slapped her on the back, but by then tears were running down her cheeks.

"You shouldn't quarrel!" she said. "You're the manor children! You've got to stick together! One for all and all for one!"

I wasn't sure if the tears came from coughing or if Gisela really was crying. And although rays of sunlight danced over the tablecloth, I was cold.

"I'm going to my room," I mumbled.

And from the stairs, I heard my mother say: "Don't worry about it, Gisela! They'll work it out! You know how kids are. By tomorrow, the fight will be forgotten!"

But my mother was wrong. We didn't forget anything. Not the next morning and not the morning after that. We made our way to school in silence, sat next to each other on the bus in silence, and carried home our failed English tests in silence. In the afternoons, Daniel and Lucas pulled one red-eye after another out of the moat while I rode around for hours in the woods or lay on the lawn counting clouds.

———

I DON'T KNOW WHOSE IDEA it was anymore. Maybe it was my mother with her new red hair or Gisela with her head scarf. I can't imagine that Peter thought it up. He mostly stayed out of things, for he knew the least about us. It had always been that way. Peter went to work in the morning and came home late in the afternoon. He took the garbage out to the bins and brought firewood in from the shed. On Saturdays, he drove to the supermarket and did the week's shopping. Whenever I saw him, he was always carrying something: a case of water, shopping bags, his briefcase, a log for the stove.

Sometimes I thought that all fathers were like that.

Fathers are there for rough work. Fathers do the heavy lifting. Fathers know how to start the lawnmower and put up shelves. Fathers patch up bike tires and know about tools. Fathers can chop down trees, but they can't plant radishes or ask questions and they can't offer comfort.

And when I thought about it like that, I didn't care anymore that my father had gone away. My mother and I, we could carry a case of water all by ourselves. And we'd managed to put up the shelves in my room on our own too.

I don't know whose idea it was anymore. I only know that I thought it was a stupid idea and that Daniel certainly wouldn't like it either. After all, we hadn't spoken to each other for two weeks.

The newspapers said it was the summer of the century, and the anchors on the network news said it was the warmest May since records had been kept. School was let out early every day due to the heat, and we were sent home after fourth period, for by ten o'clock the thermometer already showed 82 degrees in the shade.

My mother sat in front of the house under the big umbrella.

"How was school?"

"Great!"

"I have a surprise for you!" she said. "Take a guess!"

I must have made a pretty idiotic face, because my mother began to laugh out loud.

"We're going to barbecue tonight!" she said.

Yes, that sure was a surprise, since we hadn't barbecued in ages. The old grill had been rusting away in the basement for years.

"It's not worth it just for the two of us!" my mother always said when I asked. "It's too much trouble! We can fry up the sausages in a pan just as well!"

Barbecuing belonged back in the time when I was still little and had a dad who lived at home. He was in charge of the grill, he fired up the coals, and he showed me how to make stick bread—how to wrap the dough around the long stick, and how far away from the embers you have to hold it. I think my mother didn't want me to be reminded of that. And maybe she didn't want to remember it either, because the nights we barbecued were always nice. My father and my mother didn't fight then. They laughed together and sometimes they even kissed.

For a brief moment, I was really looking forward to it, and then my mother said: "Gisela and Peter are coming, too, and we're going to grill stick bread for you kids!"

My high spirits burst like a balloon pricked by a pin. I stared down at my shoes and bit my lower lip.

"Well, be a little happy about it!" said my mother. "And don't make such a face all the time!"

They came at seven. Peter carried a shopping bag of meat for the grill. My mother opened a bottle of wine. Then she gave Lucas a hug and stroked Daniel's hair.

Gisela sat down right away in the garden chair, where my mother had put an extra pillow. Gisela was completely out of breath, as if she'd just gone running, though it was barely fifty steps to our door.

I went into the kitchen to get the glasses.

"And bring the apple juice!" my mother called out.

I took my time.

When I turned around, Daniel was standing before me. I gave a start.

"What do you want?"

"To help!"

"I'll manage it myself!"

"Don't be an idiot!" Daniel tried to take the juice bottle away from me.

"I'm not an idiot! You're an idiot!" I held the bottle tight.

"Let go!" Daniel pulled on the bottle. "Let go! I'm stronger than you anyways!"

"Are not!"

"Am too!" With one tug, he tore the bottle out of my hand. "See!"

We stood opposite each other, all red in the face, and suddenly we had to laugh. We laughed so hard I nearly lost my grip on the glasses.

"You stink like fish!" I snorted.

"And you like sour grapes!" snorted Daniel.

"Are we supposed to die of thirst out here?" my mother yelled from below.

"As far as I'm concerned, you can!" I giggled.

"We're coming already!" yelled Daniel.

We went down the stairs.

"Just don't drop the bottle," I said.

"Or you the glasses!" grinned Daniel.

As I put the glasses down on the table and Daniel poured the apple juice, both Gisela and my mother smiled, but, thank god, they didn't make any comment.

Peter had fired up the coals and was putting the sausages on the grill, and Lucas was helping his father.

They told stories about before—about the time back when the pigsty was still standing, about the time back before the big fire, about the time back when the countess invited the tenant children to the manor house on Christmas Eve and every child got a present and a bagful of sweets.

"That was so long ago," said Gisela. "That was so long ago, you all were not even a spark in your parents' eyes!"

It grew dark and Peter lit the torches. My mother put lanterns on the table. Daniel, Lucas, and I were allowed to go off with three of the torches, and we ran along the black lane of chestnuts all the way down to the frog pond. An owl flew soundlessly above our heads.

Daniel took two little plastic sticks out of his pocket.

"Do you know what these are?"

I shook my head.

"These are snap lights! You need them to fish for eel!"

"How come?"

"You go fishing for eel at night, and then you snap the sticks and they start to glow. You have to tie them to the fishing line. When an eel bites, it pulls the lights under the water and then you can see where it is in the dark."

We stuck the torches into the ground and took a few steps into the darkness. Daniel snapped one of the sticks, and it really did light up. It lit up like a great big glow-worm.

"You can keep it," said Daniel.

When we came back, Gisela's chair was empty.

"Where's Mom?" asked Lucas.

"She went to bed!" Peter said. "Mom was tired!"

"Do we have to go to bed now too?" asked Lucas, and his voice was suddenly very small.

"No, you don't," said my mother. The candlelight fell over her face and made it soft. Her red hair shimmered, and I thought she looked perfectly beautiful.

"If you feel like it, you can sleep outside tonight," said

Peter. He pointed to the wide garden bench. "You two boys can lie down over there!"

Lucas jumped for joy, letting out his loudest warrior cry, and the peacocks answered at least as loudly. Daniel and I stood grinning in the candlelight.

"And you can take the lounger," said my mother. "So, go get the bedclothes and put on your pajamas. And don't forget to brush your teeth."

"And be quiet in the house!" said Peter to the boys. "Don't wake your mother!"

When I came out again, with my teeth brushed and my bedclothes under my arm, my mother was sitting alone at the table.

"Where's Peter?"

"Surprise!" giggled my mother.

I could tell from her voice that she was a little drunk.

I didn't like that, even though I knew that all grown-ups sometimes get drunk. I didn't think it was so bad with the others. My Uncle Fritz always told jokes and my grandfather imitated chickens, and in the end they always sang old folk songs: "Long, Long Ago" or "All Through the Night." And Uncle Fritz took out his wallet and gave me a five-dollar bill when he was drunk.

"You shouldn't drink so much!" I said.

"Oh, sweetie!" giggled my mother. "Must you always be so sensible? I haven't been drinking too much. Don't you worry!"

She stood up, stretched the sheet over the lounger, and fluffed up the pillow.

"You'll be snug as a bug in here!" she laughed.

"Just the same!" I said softly and held on tightly to my snap light.

As Daniel and Lucas came up, we heard a loud splash in the moat.

"Well, finally!" said my mother.

"What are you two up to?" I asked.

"We're taking a boat ride!"

Daniel and I exchanged looks.

"I want to come too!" cried Lucas.

"Absolutely not!" said my mother. "This boat ride is just for grown-ups!" She fluffed up the other pillows and smoothed out the sheets.

"And what if you fall in?" cried Lucas.

"Then we'll call real loud and you can come save us!" my mother laughed.

The torches had burned down. We lay under our blankets, stared up at the starry sky, and listened to the soft splashing of the oars when Peter put them in the water. Somewhere near the bushes a hedgehog coughed.

The splashing grew softer and softer. Now and again, the breeze carried my mother's laughter over the water. Peter's voice was barely audible anymore.

Daniel blew into his hands and made an owl call. It sounded incredibly real. Actually, it was supposed to have been our secret signal. I'd practiced it for months, but I always did something wrong, and finally we had to give it up. "Broads just aren't any good at that!" Daniel had said.

"Where are they now?" asked Lucas.

"On the other side of the manor," Daniel answered. "Can'cha hear?"

"No I can't!" said Lucas.

"That's my point!"

I strained to hear in the darkness. Aside from the flapping of the redeye, there wasn't a single sound. No laughter, no measured splash of oars, and no voices. A duck quacked in its sleep and far away in the woods an owl had finally heard Daniel's call and answered.

Right above us was the Big Dipper.

Maybe I couldn't do an owl call, but I sure knew my constellations. Because the ceiling above my bed was covered with fluorescent stars—a parting gift from my father. He gave me the stars three days before he left. He had spent hours standing on a ladder with a big, fat book in his hand, measuring out the distance between the stars of the northern hemisphere and sticking them precisely in their place. And in the evening, we lay next to each other in the dark and the stars glowed on the ceiling of my room, and my father had explained it all.

"Look there, that's Cassiopeia, and that's the Big Dipper, and over there, d'you see, that star all the way at the top, that's the North Star."

And then he told me about the Southern Cross, which you can only see on the other side of the world, and which is supposed to be so beautiful that it takes your breath away.

"And later, when you're big, sweet pea, then we'll take a trip there, you and I, just the two of us, and I'll show you the most beautiful night sky in the world, I promise you!"

The Big Dipper was directly above us and maybe, at that very moment, my father was also looking up at it and thinking of me.

Lucas had fallen asleep. His breathing was calm and regular.

"Are you asleep yet?" I whispered.

Daniel didn't answer.

"Hey, old man, I can hear you're awake, you know!"

Daniel sniffled.

"What's the matter? You're not crying, are you?"

"I'm not crying!" sobbed Daniel. "I never cry!"

"D'you wanna come over here?"

I heard his blankets rustling, and then he was lying next to me. His face was all wet and he clung to me and I held him tight and didn't know what to say.

I would have really liked to tell him about my father and the Southern Cross and the Big Dipper and the evening star, but I couldn't. Comfort, after all, was something our mothers were always there for. They were the ones who stuck band-aids on bleeding knees and held burned fingers under cold water and blew on them three times. I was just a kid, and all I could do was to hold Daniel tight.

And I held him tight until his crying stopped.

Then I let him go and we both looked up at the sky.

"Do you believe that God lives up there?" Daniel asked.

"I don't know. Do you?"

"I prayed, but it didn't help. Mom isn't getting better!"

"Maybe you haven't prayed hard enough!"

"I can't do it any harder!"

I knew that Daniel was right. I'd prayed, too, when my father wanted to leave. "Dear God," I had prayed. "Dear God, please make it so Daddy stays with us!" But my father left anyway.

Maybe this stuff about God was just a story they told us, like one of those stories they tell about the Easter Bunny or Santa Claus. A story that you believe in for a while, until you notice that Santa Claus has Uncle Hubert's boots on; that you believe in until you look out the window on Easter morning and see Mom hiding the chocolate eggs.

Maybe there wasn't anything up there except cold and endless space and maybe there really wasn't anything down here except for us and the dragonflies and the ducks and the owls and the bats.

"I don't believe in God anymore," said Daniel. "I only believe in the pike. In the pike-god. And that I'll manage to catch him. All by myself. And when I've done it, then Mom will get better again!"

I said nothing. There was nothing I could say, for the thought that there was no God made me feel speechless and alone. And the fact that Daniel thought so was even worse than my own doubts. But maybe he was right. Maybe there really was nothing but the pike-god.

We lay next to each other with our eyes open and listened in the darkness. After an eternity had passed, we heard the soft splashing of the oars. Peter said something we couldn't make out, but my mother laughed and I'd seldom been so happy to hear her laughter.

"I'm gonna go back over there, then," said Daniel and stood up. "Otherwise they'll think we were kissing!"

"You're an idiot," I giggled.

"And you're a dingbat. And don't you dare tell anyone that I was crying!"

"Not a word!"

"You swear?"

"I swear!"

I pretended to be asleep when my mother bent over me. She straightened out the blanket and gave me a kiss on the forehead, and when I blinked I saw that she did the same thing with Daniel and Lucas.

We went to the tackle shop together. Daniel, Lucas, and I. My mother drove. She tried to find a place to park and sweated and smoked and ranted out loud to herself.

"What complete idiots!" she ranted. "They must've won their driver's licenses in the lottery! Just look at that one! What on earth is she doing?"

My mother slapped her forehead with her palm. "I always knew it: women shouldn't be allowed behind the wheel!"

Daniel and I grinned.

"But you're one yourself!"

"True, but I know how to drive!"

She spun the steering wheel suddenly around and, with tires squealing, shot backward into a parking space. The man in the car behind us slammed on his brakes and gave us the finger.

I was ashamed, but Daniel whistled admiringly through the gap between his teeth.

"Slick!" he said. "No one besides my dad can manage that!"

My mother laughed loudly.

I found it embarrassing to drive with her. She always ranted like that. The others were always the idiots. I could still remember a time years ago, when we were driving on vacation.

My father had sat next to her with his lips pressed tightly together and there was an icy silence in the car.

"I'm just not passenger material!" my mother claimed. "Now would you finally let me drive!"

And she kept on nagging at him until my father stopped the car and angrily slammed the door. After that she drove and he was allowed to fill up the tank.

And one time, on a trip to Denmark, when he spilled a couple drops of gas on his sandals, she jumped out of the car sputtering with irritation and roared: "The man can't even pump gas!"

People stared at us with snide grins and I wished I were invisible.

I was ashamed, Daniel whistled through his teeth, and then we were standing in front of the shop. Angler

Heaven—Your Source for Fishing Supplies.

I can still recall the smell in there perfectly. It smelled of iron and dust and mealworms. And things were glittering all over the place. There were spoon baits and little metal fish that looked as real as our redeye. There were soft, neon-bright wiggle-worms and fishing line and lead sinkers and swivels and bobbers.

It reminded me of the goodie bags that fat Uncle Ewald with the cigar always brought. All this colorful, shiny tackle junk would have fit right in with the stuff in those goodie bags. Along with the sticky Cracker Jacks I'd find bright wiggle-worms and little fuzzy caterpillars that you could pull along the table by a string.

Daniel and Lucas had long since disappeared into the rows of high shelves. From time to time they emerged again and my mother had to examine one hand net after another.

When it came to me, she never had that much patience. She always hurried me along. Especially in shoe stores.

"Haven't you made up your mind yet? Well, get a move on, then, you snail! We don't want to stay here all night!" And then I'd pick the blue shoes, although I actually wanted the red ones.

In Angler Heaven, I could have made up my mind quickly. To me, all hand nets looked alike. I drummed my fingers impatiently on the counter and my mother gave me a reproachful look.

The hand net was nothing more than a great big tea filter with a telescoping handle, and the bait trap was a square net stretched over a frame of plastic tubes. Each of the four corners had a rope attached above to a ring. I could have come up with that idea myself, and then we wouldn't have had to fool around with Gisela's plastic bucket for three weeks.

Bait trap, hand net—I'd always imagined these words to mean something entirely different, something out of the ordinary, something that I would never in my life have been able to think up for myself. In Angler Heaven, I understood for the first time that fishing lingo was just a secret language, and I realized that I had to learn this language if I wanted to have my say.

Of course, we tried out the trap right away. Daniel slid it into the water and pulled it up. And indeed, we hauled seven redeye out at once. It was ridiculously easy and I was happy that the redeye didn't have to swallow hooks any more. Daniel threw the fish back into the water.

"Are you crazy?" cried Lucas. "Without the baitfish, you'll never catch the pike!"

"We're not even allowed to catch him yet," said Daniel.

"And why not?"

"Because it's not pike season yet. We have to wait until July!"

"Who says?"

"The earl!"

"I don't believe you!" said Lucas. "I think you're just chicken!"

Daniel didn't answer. He simply folded the trap up and went inside the house.

I wasn't sure whether Daniel was telling the truth, but I knew for sure that I was relieved, for I'd imagined what it would be like when he killed the pike. And I knew I didn't want to see it.

WHILE THE BLOOMS FADED AWAY in the mustard field, summer gained strength and my red-headed mother stood smoking at the stove, making strawberry jam.

"How was school?"

"Great!"

She stood with her back to me. With one hand, she stirred the jam and with the other, she held her cigarette. I watched her and waited for the ashes to fall into the pot of jam, but it didn't happen.

"There's something for you on the table!" she said without turning around. "From Gisela!"

It was a small rectangular package. It was gift-wrapped and tied with a red ribbon.

I held it in my hand, turned it this way and that, and tried to guess what it could be. It felt like a book.

"Well, open it already!" my mother prodded. "Don't you even want to know what it is?"

Of course I wanted to know what it was, but after all, it was so much nicer to try to guess first.

"You're just like your father!" my mother said.

"And you're nosy!"

"Don't be fresh again!"

Whenever my mother got a present, she tore the ribbon right off and shredded the paper to pieces. She simply couldn't wait to see what she was getting.

I found that awful, especially when I'd tried hard to wrap a present up nicely.

My father always used to hold his presents for a long time. He would feel them all around, carefully shake them, turn them round and round, and only then gently untie the knots and remove the Scotch tape. My mother would make fun of him and impatiently spur him on. But I always thought it was nice that he took so much care.

"Well, go on, what is it?" asked my mother.

She licked the wooden spoon clean and came over next to me. I didn't want her to be the first to see what Gisela had given me. I fiddled with the tape.

"Oh, I can't even watch!" groaned my mother.

I ignored her. Carefully, I unfolded the wrapping paper. It really was a book. *The Beginner's Guide to Fishing,* I read.

"Let's see!" said my mother. She was about to grab the book from my hand, but just at that moment the jam boiled over, and she cursed and ran to the stove.

I fled to my room. There, I turned the book over and read the blurb on the back. "All the beginner needs to know in a nutshell," I read. "*The Beginner's Guide to Fishing* is a concise and knowledgeable introduction to the sport, written by a practitioner for practical use. The book provides the beginner with all the information necessary for angling. And even for the experienced angler, it is a treasure trove of dependable information about fishing waters, fish, tackle, fishing methods, and much more."

I opened the book up, and that's where I found the letter.

Anna, my dear girl!

I wish I could be there now and see your face when you open this book. You probably think I should have given it to Daniel. For I know full well what you think of fishing. And believe me, I'd rather see the fish alive in an aquarium myself. But you know how boys are, and you also know that we can't stop those two from going fishing, because when they're fishing, it takes their minds off everything else for a while.

I don't want you all fighting about it. On the contrary, I would like it if you could join them too. You've always done everything together, after all. You went to kindergarten together and I'm sure you remember your first day of school together. And do you still remember how you built the tree house? Actually, you three have grown up like siblings, and I would like it to stay that way. Especially now that I'm sick, it would be good to know that you're getting along.

Dear Anna, I know that this is a big wish.
But I also know that you're a wonderful girl. I've
always wanted a daughter like you. So, my dear
girl, read the fishing book and show the two how
to do it right. And maybe someday, you'll have
just as much fun fishing for the pike as Daniel and
Lucas!

I send you a big, warm hug.
Your Gisela

That was the first and only letter I ever got from Gisela.

And I would have promised her anything. Perhaps because she called me her dear girl, perhaps because I hoped it would make her better, and perhaps because Daniel was right and there really was a pike god who was all-powerful and could work miracles if you delivered him from eternal life.

I heard my mother's footsteps on the stairs and hid Gisela's letter under my pillow. Without a word, I handed her the book. She flipped through it and shook her head.

"And don't you forget to thank her!" she said.

The book was my secret. I showed it neither to Daniel nor to Lucas and read it every night. I already knew that the season for pike fishing started on May 1. But I didn't say anything, and luckily Lucas didn't find anyone to ask.

Mondays and Fridays, when Lucas was at soccer practice, Daniel walked alone across the courtyard with the trap. I watched him in secret from the window.

I saw how he repeatedly sunk the trap into the water and pulled it up. I saw how he grabbed a redeye and tried to hold it. I counted the seconds. It was never more than ten before he let go again in disgust. I saw how, afterward, he hung over the parapet and had to retch.

I felt sorry for Daniel and at the same time I admired him.

Once, my father had told me: "When you're afraid of something, you have to look right at it first and then you have to touch it. And when you've managed that, your fear is all gone. Remember that, sweet pea!"

That was the day the big German shepherd had lunged at me and I'd run for my life and couldn't stop screaming. My father had taken me in his arms and told me that. But I never have managed to look right at a German shepherd and then touch it. At some point, I gave up trying and knew I'd have to spend the rest of my life being afraid.

But Daniel was different. He didn't give up. I was sure that he would manage it.

Having to go and thank Gisela weighed on me like a stone. Every evening, my mother asked about it, and every evening I answered: "Not yet, but tomorrow for sure."

And my mother grumbled and called me ungrateful. "I can certainly understand that you're not pleased with the fishing book, but you could at least say thank you! It's the proper thing to do!"

It was the proper thing to do, but I was scared.

I was scared of seeing Gisela. I was scared of hearing her cough, scared of having to hug her. I didn't want to go inside that silent house, where the blinds were always down. I was afraid of the smell in there, and of the ticking of the clock. And most of all, I was afraid of the oxygen tank.

I'd been sitting up in the climbing tree with Daniel when Peter drove into the courtyard. We both watched him lug the tank into the house.

"What's that thing for?" I asked, but Daniel had only shrugged his shoulders.

The oxygen tank looked just like the helium tanks for filling up the brightly colored balloons at the fair, which I never could hold on to when I was little. The balloons always flew up into the sky, and when I cried, my father would laugh and say: "The angels are playing with them now."

I couldn't talk about it with Daniel, but on the way to school, Lucas explained that the oxygen tank was for his mom.

"It helps my mom breathe better, and then she'll get better, too!" And he giggled and took my hand. "You know what? Mom's oxygen mask is really just like the ones on the airplane! It really is!" And he was proud of it.

No, I did not want to go inside that house, I didn't want to see the mask, or Gisela either, and I felt guilty for it.

But each night, I read the fishing guide and found out everything there is to know about the pike.

"The pike is perhaps the most popular predatory fish among serious anglers," I read. "It came by this title not least because of its fighting spirit. But its flesh, too, is generally considered to be a delicacy. The pike is very demanding concerning its environment. It prefers still, shallow areas near the shore and slow flowing waters with green banks. It is considered to be a typical 'lie-in-wait' fish and loner."

While reading this, it occurred to me that the pike and Daniel were actually quite similar. Two loners on an estate surrounded by water, Daniel and the pike, and both lay in wait for their prey. One breathed air and the other breathed water, but even that made them the same, for both would suffocate if they were to trade places.

I read that you have to knock the pike out with a blow to the head first, and then put a knife through its head. I read that if you cut a pike's heart out, it can keep on beating for twenty minutes more. And I imagined what that would feel like.

I saw myself holding in my hand a pike's heart that simply went on beating.

In the night, while storm clouds passed over the manor, I dreamt. I grew gills and my legs were transformed

into tail fins. I let myself sink down to the bottom of the moat. And there, deep below, where everything was still and black and impenetrable, I swam after the pike, froze motionless when he lay in wait for his prey, and then darted with him, swift as an arrow and open-mouthed, at the redeye. I felt light, I was quick and agile, and the water protected me. Behind the ivy, which grew down deep into the water, was the entrance to the pike's castle. And in my dream, I could swim inside and find magnificent halls and chambers, and when I looked up, I saw the clouds and the stars mirrored in the transparent ceiling of the rooms. The pike nodded to me, and I saw him freeze, saw a slow redeye pulling away above him, noticed the fishing line, but it was already too late. My voice was gone in the water. I couldn't scream to warn him. I saw his struggle, saw how he tried to break the line, saw how he reared himself up, again and again, while the hook worked its way deeper and deeper into his flesh.

It was a clap of thunder that finally woke me from this dream. But I couldn't stop screaming until my mom came, put her arms around me, and rocked me like she did when I was little.

WHEN A THUNDERSTORM came through, the sky first turned yellow and then dark. The air was heavy and sticky. The wind was still, not a leaf moved on the climbing tree. We just sat in the branches and waited. On the stone bridge, the bucket with the redeye catch still stood on the parapet.

For more than a week now, they'd been testing their courage. That's what they called the new game Daniel had come up with.

"Whoever can hold on to the redeye the longest is the winner!" he said.

"Well, then, you'd better brace yourself!" Lucas giggled. "'Cause that's a game you'll never win!"

"Wait and see!" grinned Daniel.

He pulled Gisela's stopwatch out of his pants pocket and gave it to me.

"You keep the time!"

I was happy to play referee, because the mere thought of having to hold the slimy fish in my own hands made me ill.

Daniel showed me what button to push to stop the timer, and then threw the trap into the water and pulled it back up.

It was a stupid game, for hardly any redeye came out of the competition alive.

"Holy cow!" said Lucas at last. "Holy cow! My dumb brother really can hold a fish!"

And Daniel grinned and spit into the water.

When the sky turned yellow and dark, we climbed up into the tree. I thought this was dangerous, since trees are the very place where lightning strikes, but Daniel only laughed and said I could always go home and crawl into bed. Besides, he claimed to be invincible, because anyone who can hold a redeye can't be hit by lightning.

At the first roll of thunder, my mother opened the window.

"Daniel," she called, "come inside already! And bring your brother and Anna!"

I was startled, for Gisela had always been the one who'd call us. It was the first time my mother had ever called like that, and I saw that it made Daniel flinch as well.

We jumped down from the tree and ran to the house just as the first raindrops fell.

She stood in the doorway and waited for us. I saw right away that she was annoyed.

"You must have lost your minds!" she railed. "What could you possibly be thinking, climbing up into a tree when the lightning flares up? Haven't you learned anything? We all know that boys are daredevils! But you," she bellowed, "I expected more from you! You're a girl, after all, and the oldest, to boot!"

My mother had seized me by the arm while she railed at us, and with every phrase, I felt her hard fingertips dig tighter into my flesh.

I quickly tore myself loose and ran up the stairs. I slammed the door shut and threw myself on the bed.

Why was she so unfair?

Why was it always my fault?

Why did she never have a kind word to say to me?

I was her only child, after all.

Whenever I wanted to give her a hug, she laughed and pushed me aside. "You're cutting off my air! Don't be so emotional all the time!"

But emotional is what I was, especially when I wanted to show her how much I loved her. I only wanted for her to show me that, too. But that's something she did very rarely.

I wanted so much to be like her, but she always said: "You're just like your father!"

Maybe that's why she acted that way with me.

Once I even heard her tell Gisela how much she'd wanted a boy. He would have been called Jan, but then I turned out to be just an Anna.

"And just imagine," she'd said to Gisela. "Just imagine, now I have to go through everything I experienced myself as a girl, all over again . . . the standoffishness . . . the defiance . . . the lies . . . everything . . . oh, I wish she'd been a boy!"

I can't remember what Gisela replied anymore, but I remember perfectly how much it hurt to hear it. From then on, I knew that nothing I did would be right for my mother. I would always be just a girl. Although I could do anything boys could do. I could even pee in an arc. But that didn't count for my mother. And now that Gisela was sick, she suddenly had two boys. It was as simple as that.

As I lay on the bed sobbing into the pillow I could hear my mother laughing down in the kitchen. And Lucas and Daniel were laughing with her.

I flinched as I suddenly felt a hand on my shoulder.

"No crying allowed!" said Daniel.

"Why do you always have to sneak around like that?"

"Because I'm not a hippopotamus!"

"Leave me alone!"

"Not a chance!"

He sat on the edge of my bed.

"Why are you crying?"

"Because . . . it's none of your business!"

"Sure it is! Now go on and tell me!"

"Because . . . because it's always my fault! Because I can't do anything right for her! Because she's always carping at me! Because she likes you much better . . . to say nothing of Lucas! And because I can't stand it anymore!"

He stroked my back and said nothing and then he pulled a creased stick of gum out of his pants pocket and put it down next to my head.

"You can have it! It's cinnamon flavor! From America!"

I lifted my head and looked at him.

"Really?"

"Really!"

He gave me a lopsided grin and I saw that he was embarrassed.

"And the other thing?" I asked. "The thing about my mother?"

He shrugged. "I know all about that! It's the same at our house! I'm always to blame, too, never Lucas! It's probably normal!"

"Maybe we got switched at the hospital when we were babies? Maybe we're in the wrong families? Do you think that, too, sometimes?"

He nodded and blushed.

"Maybe," he said. "Maybe my real mother lives some-where else entirely . . . maybe my real mother is healthy and runs across the courtyard to the office every day. Across a different courtyard, on another estate . . ."

THE SUNFLOWERS GREW in front of our kitchen window.

I hadn't seen Gisela since the night of our barbecue. She was in the process of simply disappearing. Just like the yellow of the mustard had disappeared, and the red of the poppies. Just like the little white chamomile blossoms would disappear, and after that the summer lilac.

The things we find beautiful never stay that way. Even the water had changed its color. It was now summer green and cloudy. The air shimmered with the heat.

My mother hung wet bedsheets in front of the win-dow. But she didn't do it until the evening, after return-ing, sad and exhausted, from Gisela's bedside. But first, she opened the fridge, took out the vodka bottle, poured, and emptied the glass in one gulp.

I stood in the doorway to the kitchen and watched her. Watched her push her red hair back from her fore-head, watched her shudder as the liquor went down.

"How was it at Gisela's?" I asked, because I felt like I had to say something.

"Don't ask!" she answered.

"Just tell me!"

And then she told me. She told me about Gisela's breathing, about the oxygen mask and the loud hissing that accompanied every breath. She told me that Gisela slept most of the time, or maybe just kept her eyes closed, because breathing was so loud and difficult. She told me they'd talked about the past, about the time when I was born, and then Daniel. And how cold the winter had been.

My first winter, and Daniel's too.

"And we wanted to take some pictures of you, so we just stuck you upright into the snow. It was so high that you couldn't tip over, much less run away!"

My mother chuckled.

"And in the afternoons, we used to put you in the baby bouncers, 'cause bouncing was supposed to be good for your back muscles. And you just lay there stiff as a board with fear and didn't move a muscle. But Daniel, he got the knack of it right away and kept swinging his arms about until the bouncer tipped over! Just tipped right over! Oh, but you should have seen Gisela. She wrote such a furious letter to the company. Consumer Product Safety seal, my foot. The bouncer's more likely to get a baby killed. And then the company had sent her a swing as compensation! Just imagine, the most expensive baby swing in the catalog! For free!"

My mother's chuckling had turned into gurgling laughter and I had to laugh along. I laughed and didn't ask what I actually wanted to ask her. It was the question I was thinking about the entire time, the question that hung over this summer like a great, black thundercloud.

"Mom," I didn't ask. "Mom, is Gisela going to get well again?"

No, I didn't ask.

But as she talked, my sad mother became my happy mother again, and hope grew in me along with the sunflowers in front of our kitchen window.

In the morning, the bedsheets in front of the windows were dry and stiff.

The young wild ducks had quacked loudly the whole night. And I had lain awake for a long time trying to understand what they were saying. Mostly, it sounded like quarreling, as if one was shouting to the other: "I can do it better than you can!" But sometimes is also sounded tender and sleepy. In my head, I divided up the ducks into boys and girls. The loud ones were the boys. And the girls said: "Hush up now, we're tired!"

My father used to tell me stories like that. Evenings, in bed. The story about the long-necked bird that's lost its way and sits in the rushes calling for its mother over and over.

"D'you hear it? Now he's calling again!"

I strained to hear in the black night and heard a lonesome, wailing whistle.

Or he told the story of the great white superfrog who appears to the pond frogs at night.

"And when he comes, sweet pea, then the green pond frogs begin to sing in chorus. That's their hymn of worship.

D'you hear? They're singing now. Now, the great white superfrog is standing at the edge of the pond and they're greeting him!"

I strained to hear in the black night and, indeed, the frogs were singing a chorale.

But best of all, I liked the story about the yahoos, who copied everything they saw.

"They don't know how to sing. But if one of them starts up a song, then all the others sing along. D'you hear? They're singing now."

I strained to hear in the black night and, indeed, strains of a song wafted over from the shooting club gathering in the village.

My father would have liked my duck story, too, I'm sure.

DANIEL AND LUCAS WERE at our house every afternoon now.

And my mother did things she'd never done before. On a completely ordinary Tuesday, she stood in the kitchen mixing waffle batter. Normally, she only did that on Christmas or my birthday. Then, and only then, were there ever waffles with warm fruit syrup and whipped cream.

"It begins when you sink in his arms . . . It ends with your arms in his sink," proclaimed a postcard pinned to the kitchen bulletin board.

"Don't you go grousing all the time!" she said when I asked her why she was making waffles.

"I'm glad to do it, and Daniel and Lucas are looking forward to it. It wouldn't kill you to be happy once in a while, either, you know!"

When we came home from school now, it smelled like lunch in the courtyard outside. It smelled like lasagna, or fish sticks, or breaded cutlets with peas and carrots. And that was new too. Before, she never used to cook until the evening.

"Because it's much more practical," she'd explained. "That way, I can plan my day better, and you're certainly capable of making yourself a sandwich in the afternoon!"

Before, our fridge was only well-stocked when my mother was on a special diet. That's the only time she ever cooked regularly in the afternoon, and put a dab of butter in the low-fat dishes for me.

But now, Daniel and Lucas sat at our kitchen table, and Before was over.

My mother cooked and baked like there was no tomorrow, and we scraped out the mixing bowls. We hardly had a chance to take the first bite before she'd ask how it was, and when Daniel, with his mouth full, said "Yummy!" she beamed.

In truth, I'd always wanted just such a mother. An aproned mother who would smell of vanilla. An aproned mother who would make chocolate pudding whenever I had a problem. Who would say: "Have something to eat first, and then you'll feel better!" and put sausages and broccoli with cheese sauce on my plate when I messed up my English homework.

I'd always wanted just such a mother, and now she was standing in our kitchen and I didn't know whether I should be happy about it.

Everything was changing and I just wanted for things to always stay the way they were.

I think Daniel felt the same.

In the mornings, when we climbed into the school bus, the village children huddled together and whispered.

And three days before the end of the school year, Klaus Stelter's little brother suddenly pointed his finger at Daniel and said loudly: "My mom said his mom's gonna die soon!"

At that, Daniel sprang up, pushed past me, and flung himself on Klaus Stelter's little brother.

I tried to hold him back. "Let it go! He's much smaller than you!"

But Daniel wasn't listening. He held the little boy in a headlock and panted: "Go on! Say it again!"

And Klaus Stelter's little brother burst out crying and sputtered: "I take it all back! It's not true! It was just a joke! I take it all back!"

The snickering and the whispering had stopped. The bus was eerily still.

We all held our breath and stared at Daniel, his face flushed and distorted with rage, who held the little Stelter in a clinch. Not even the bus driver moved. Everyone seemed frozen in place.

"Dear God!" I prayed. "Dear God, please make Daniel stop!"

But Daniel only squeezed harder and the little Stelter panted and gasped for air like a redeye out of water.

It was Anna-Sofia Schulze-Wettering who came out of the trance first. She gave me a nudge.

"He's gonna break his neck! You're his friend! Quick, say something to make him let go!"

I looked into her face. She had pale blue eyes and freckles. I don't know why, but I suddenly thought of the dead cat, and that spring kittens always had pale blue eyes, too, at first, to say nothing of nine lives.

How I'd always wished that she would speak to me. How I'd wished that Anna-Sofia would be my friend. And of all times, she chose to speak to me now, when I would have rather the earth swallowed me up right then and there on Daniel's account.

And she gave me a shake, and said again: "Quick! You have to do something! You're the only one who can do something!"

The bus driver had gotten up and was coming down the aisle with a heavy step.

I didn't know what I should say, but then again, I did.

"Daniel!" I called out. "Daniel, think of the pike!"

He looked at me as if he were coming back from somewhere far away, somewhere no one had gone before him. He looked at me as if he didn't know who I was anymore.

"Please, Daniel!" I said.

And then he let go.

Klaus Stelter's little brother fell back and snot ran out his nose and he went on gasping for air. He rubbed his neck.

"Where d'you think you are? There'll be no fighting on my bus! You get back to your seats right now, you hooligans!" railed the bus driver. "And in the future, you'd best behave yourselves!"

With the same heavy step, he went back to the driver's seat.

Anna-Sofia Schulze-Wettering flashed a fresh grin and winked at me, as though the two of us had a secret.

"You can come over sometime, if you feel like it!"

Just four weeks ago, I would have been ecstatic about this invitation. My knees would have gone weak, and my heart would have beat wildly. I would have said "yes" and "I'd love to come." But today, it seemed to me it would be a betrayal of Daniel to visit Anna-Sofia. Maybe because she'd winked at me like that.

Daniel sat next to me, his head hung low, just staring in front of him. He'd gone all pale and I wanted to take his hand, but that wasn't possible, because between us was an invisible wall.

I looked out the window. Outside, the fields and the farms and the hedges flew by.

The others were talking among themselves again, but the motor droned so loudly that I couldn't understand a thing. And actually, I didn't even want to understand, because I already knew what they were talking about.

In front of the school, we waited until everyone else

had gotten off the bus. I heard the school bell ring.

"Well, hurry up, you two!" said the bus driver. "You don't want to be late, do you?"

Daniel shuffled along slowly behind me. At the entrance to the school, he suddenly stood still.

"I don't care what you do, but I'm not going in there!"

"Don't be a fool! You'll just get in trouble!"

"So what . . . you go then!"

Daniel sat on the wall that separated the school yard from the garden. I looked at him sitting there and I knew that he meant it. I also knew that I couldn't leave him alone, not for anything in the world.

"Well, come on, then," I said and pulled him down from the wall. "We can't stay here. Everyone can see us."

He let himself be pulled along and I led him under the dense, leafy canopy of the weeping beech that stood in the garden. Before, we used to hide there during recess, when we wanted to mess with the village kids.

"You shouldn't squabble with others!" Gisela always said. "And if they bother you, just avoid them!"

The weeping beech was our secret hiding place, until one day that stopped, too, and we didn't have a secret place anymore.

But now, here we were again, leaning back against the smooth trunk, just like we used to back then. And the leafy tent reached all the way down to the ground, and the light was just like it used to be, dim and green and familiar.

We heard the sssrrrii-sssrrrii of the swallows and

the wind carried over scraps of song from the music room "...oh, the summertime has come, and the trees are sweetly bloomin'..." and then Daniel suddenly said: "Maybe it's true, what Stelter said. Maybe everyone knows, everyone, except for us!"

I gave a start.

"My mom has cancer," said Daniel.

"How long have you known?"

"A long time. I'm not stupid, am I?"

He looked at me.

"And don't you pretend you haven't known for a long time too."

I swallowed and nodded.

"But your mother can get better again!" I said. "My mother said that there's many people who get better!"

"D'you know any?" asked Daniel.

I shook my head.

"I don't want my mom to die!"

Daniel sprang up and then he suddenly screamed: "I DON'T WANT IT!" he screamed. "I DON'T WANT IT! I DON'T WANT IT! I DON'T WANT IT!"

And with each I DON'T WANT IT he slammed his head in time against the tree trunk, and then he turned his back to me and cried.

There are moments you know you'll never forget. Even when you want to forget them. And while Daniel was still slamming his forehead against the tree trunk, I knew that this was such a moment.

I wanted to hold Daniel tight and couldn't.

I wanted to say something and couldn't.

I wanted to run away and couldn't.

I couldn't even cry.

Daniel was the first to speak.

He still stood with his back turned to me.

"Do you remember the night of the barbecue?" he asked.

"Yeah," I said.

"You know how we were talking about God?"

"Why?"

"Because I've thought about it!"

"And?"

"If there's no God, then he doesn't care if we believe in him or not. And then, he can't be angry and punish us for not believing in him. But he can't help us either, if he doesn't exist."

"You mean, there'd be no point at all in praying?"

"Completely no point, and it's no help, either!"

I suddenly had the feeling that the ground swayed beneath my feet. If what Daniel said was right, then everything I'd believed up to that point was wrong. Everything that my mother had told me, everything my grandmother had made me believe, was false. If what Daniel said was right, then there would be no more guardian angels and no more miracles. Of course, I sometimes had my doubts about God, but it always made me feel so lost that I tried to think about something else real quick.

My thoughts had never looked anything like Daniel's thoughts. And I resisted, because once again, something else was going to change.

"And what about the guardian angels and the miracles?" I asked. "There's gotta be something for people to believe in! Otherwise you just couldn't bear it all!"

Daniel gave a short laugh. It wasn't a real laugh. It sounded more like a sob.

"You can forget about miracles, and guardian angels, too! That's all just a bunch of hooey! But I do believe in something: I believe in the pike! I believe that when I catch him, my mom will get better again."

He turned around to face me and I started. His forehead was grazed and bloody. It had to have hurt, but it didn't seem to bother him.

I pulled a handkerchief out of my pants and was about to dab the blood from his brow.

"You better not wet that with your tongue!" Daniel said. "And you better not tell anyone what happened here! I just slipped and fell, you got that? I slipped and fell, and hit my forehead."

This all happened on June 29th.

Later on, they said it was the hottest June day on record. Just before the highway overpass, Lucas caught up with us.

"What happened to you?" he asked, and pointed to Daniel's forehead.

Daniel stayed silent.

"He fell down," I said.

Lucas shook his head.

There was a car in front of Daniel's house. It was black, and as we came nearer, Lucas spied the MD on the plates.

"Something's happened!" said Daniel, and started to run. As he was about to unlock the door, it opened from the inside, and my mother stepped out into the sun. She stood in front of Daniel and Lucas and blocked their way.

"You can't go in there now!" she said and put her hands on both their shoulders.

"But I want to see my mom!" said Lucas, and his voice trembled. "I have to show Mom my math homework!"

My mother pushed Lucas and Daniel gently but decisively down the front steps.

"That's not possible just now! You come on home with us for a bit first!"

Daniel lowered his head and I began to feel scared.

We put our schoolbags in the hall and followed my mother into the kitchen. She got three bowls out of the cabinet and filled them with vegetable soup from the pot on the stove. Then she put the bowls on the kitchen table.

"Sit down!" she said.

My heart started pounding, for she didn't ask: "How was school?" She didn't even ask what happened to Daniel's forehead. And that's the first thing she would have asked, otherwise. I was sure of that.

Daniel and Lucas sat across from me at the head of the table. My mother sat next to me. We held our spoons in our hands, but we didn't eat. We waited for her to say something.

Please, Mom, say something already! I thought, and as if she'd read my mind, my mother took a deep breath, looked at Daniel and Lucas, and then she cleared her throat and spoke.

I can still recall perfectly that there were little green peas and orange cubes of carrot swimming in the soup. And that the doves were cooing loudly outside.

I remember the midday cries of the peacocks and the tractor that came clattering over the wooden bridge. And over and over again, I see how Daniel and Lucas put their faces into their bowls. Just like that, at the same time. And then they lifted their heads up and a little green pea rolled slowly down Daniel's cheek like a small green tear. I can remember all that.

But I don't remember how my mother said *it*.

How she said that Gisela would die.

How she said that there was no more hope.

How she said that she was sorry.

The first thing I can hear her saying is that Gisela is sleeping now, and we shouldn't disturb her, and Peter would come home soon and the doctor would stay until then.

And then she says to both of them: "Go wash up!" And she clears the table and dumps the soup right back into the pot, even though their faces were just in it. And I can see that my mother's hands are shaking.

Afterward, we drove together to the ice cream shop and she bought us the biggest ice cream in the world. That's what she'd said in the car, over and over again, as if she had to get her courage up.

"I'm going to buy us the biggest ice cream in the whole world! I'm getting the biggest ice cream in the world, for sure!" And she'd tried to laugh.

That afternoon, Daniel and Lucas didn't pull any redeye out of the water. That afternoon, my mother had pulled down the blinds and blocked the summer out. She had smoked one cigarette after another.

And we had plopped ourselves down in front of the TV and eaten our ice cream with three spoons out of the big salad bowl and watched some fantasy film, and during the commercial Daniel suddenly started to sing along with the mortgage bank jingle, loudly and off key: "Your future's safe as houses." And Lucas had giggled.

That afternoon, I would have loved to sit in my mother's lap. But when I moved closer to her, she moved away, pulled her knees up to her chin, and lit another cigarette.

When Peter's car pulled into the court, my mother took Lucas and Daniel over.

"It might get late!" she had said. "If you're still hungry, make yourself a sandwich. And don't wait up, just go to bed!"

At that, she stroked my hair, but more like the way you pet a dog in passing.

I stood at the window and watched the three of them go across the court. My mother walked in the middle, her red hair glowing in the evening sun. Daniel was to her right and Lucas to her left. And my mother had put an arm around each one's shoulder, just like a real mother does. And suddenly, I thought of a fairy tale that my father used to read to me when he tucked me in. "And Brother-dear took Sister-dear by the hand and said: 'The dog under the table has it better than us. God forbid our mother ever knew of it!'"

I don't believe I ever longed for my father more than I did that evening. I longed for his deep voice, I longed for his soft belly. I longed for the smell of his aftershave and I longed for his stories.

I even longed for the stupid saying that used to make me so embarrassed. "Beans, beans, the magical fruit; the more you eat, the more you toot!"

Every time he said it, my mother drew her breath in sharply through her nose and shook her head, because that sort of thing was just so vulgar.

"Consider the child, Paul."

But my father would only laugh and then say it again.

I lay in my bed and said the rhyme out loud to myself: "Beans, beans, the magical fruit; the more you eat, the more you toot!"

And it really helped! After the fifth time, I actually had to laugh, and suddenly it was a little bit as if my dad was finally home again.

———

THE NEXT MORNING, as we walked to the bus stop, everything was almost the same as always. Lucas kicked along an empty cola can and Daniel smelled of sleep. The sun shone brightly and the light shimmered over the faded mustard field. It would be hot again, they'd said on the radio while I emptied the cereal bowl my mother had set down in front of me.

"Hurry up!" she'd said. "You need to go!"

I saw that her eyes were all swollen, but I didn't want to ask. And it was only almost the same as always, because as we walked across the highway overpass, Daniel suddenly began to sing. The trucks roared by beneath us and Daniel sang: "Your future's safe as houses!" He'd never done that before, and when I asked him why, he grinned sheepishly and said: "I just can't get it out of my head!"

We went on in silence. As we were passing by the Heitkamp cottages, Daniel suddenly burst out: "And I'm not going in there!"

"Going in where?"

"In my mom's room! I'm not going in there!"

"Me neither!" cried out Lucas, and ran after the cola can. "I'm not going in there either! Your mother wants us to go in there to tell Mommy good night, but we won't do it, and she can't make us. She's not our mother!"

"And what does Peter say?" I asked.

"Daddy said your mother should stay out of it!" cried Lucas. He kicked the can forward really far and ran off after it again.

Daniel said nothing more, but I saw that his hands had tightened into fists.

I thought what Peter had said about my mom was unfair. After all, she was the one who took care of Lucas and Daniel the whole time. She helped Lucas with his homework in the afternoon. She drove Daniel to English tutoring in the next village over. And Peter was hardly ever there, in any case. He came home later and later every evening.

"He's just like your father, that one. Hiding in his office!" Mom had said. "And if you ever need him, he's working overtime!"

And I also didn't think it right that Daniel and Lucas didn't even want to tell Gisela good night. I felt sorry for Gisela. And maybe that's why my mom had been crying.

But in the afternoon, my mother was laughing again.

"How was school?"

"Great!"

She dumped the spaghetti into the colander and stirred the tomato sauce. Then she wiped her fingers on her new apron and said to Daniel and Lucas: "You father and I, we came up with something! Something for your mom! You know that her bed stands under the window, and for weeks now, your mom's had nothing to look at except the wardrobe. She's never complained, but it must be pretty boring all the same, always having to look at a wardrobe. So today we hung a great big mirror on it. It wasn't easy to find the right angle, but we did it! Now your mom can see the courtyard from her bed! You can't imagine how happy it made her! She laughed and said: "Now I can finally see what my boys are up to! They shouldn't think I don't know what's going on, just because I'm stuck here in this bed all the time!"

For a moment, there was total silence in our kitchen. I saw that Daniel bit his lower lip. That's what I always did to stop myself from crying.

Lucas looked thoughtful and then said very slowly: "So . . . if Mom can see us in the courtyard . . . then there must be a place in the yard . . . where we could see Mom in the mirror, too!"

He nudged Daniel in the ribs with his elbow. "C'mon, bro, we gotta go try that out!"

He pulled Daniel along behind him, ran out of the kitchen, and with a great clatter, the two were down the stairs.

"And what about your lunch?" my mother yelled. But she got no answer.

Mom laughed, then put her arm around me, and we looked out the window and watched Lucas and Daniel running around the courtyard.

Suddenly, they both stood still. Lucas hopped up and down and waved his arms like crazy and Daniel made faces. He thumbed his nose. He stuck out his tongue. He put his hands up to his head with his index fingers sticking up and puffed and snorted like a bull.

"Come on, sweetie! Let's eat," Mom said. "Otherwise our spaghetti's going to get cold too!"

I would have loved to make time stand still right there.

Right there, where Mom and I sat alone together at the table. Where we heard Lucas yelling outside: "She waved back! D'ja see that? Our mom waved back!"

And Daniel let off his whooping warrior cry, like he used to when he was still little.

I would have loved to make time stand still right there. Right there, where Mom had tomato sauce smeared on her nose, and I did too, and we both looked at each other and cracked up and choked with laughter and coughed until we cried.

If I'd made time stand still there, the pike would still be alive, and Gisela, too, and I would never have shoved the strawberry ice-cream cone in Anna-Sofia Schulze-Wettering's face, and our summer would never have had to end.

I would have loved to make time stand still right there, but it can't be done. Time just marches on, and evening comes, and then it's morning, and then comes a storm, and then the sun is out. That's how time is. And then one morning, the chestnuts are all lying, brown and shiny, under the trees, and then it's winter, just like that.

ANNA-SOFIA SCHULZE-WETTERING caught up with me at the school gate. She linked her arm through mine and acted like we'd always been the best of friends. That was on the day before the last day of school.

Anna-Sofia Schulze-Wettering with the pale blue kitten eyes and the freckles smelled of milk and meadows.

"I feel like going to the ice-cream shop this afternoon. D'you wanna come?"

I couldn't help but think of the biggest ice cream in the world and didn't really feel like going, but I said anyway: "Sure, I'd love to. What time?"

"How about three?"

"Sure," I said. "That'd be fine!"

"We could go to my house afterward," Anna-Sofia said. "We have new kittens again, y'know. They're so sweet! You've just gotta see 'em! Well, then, three o'clock at the ice-cream shop!"

In her yellow summer dress, she looked like a great big butterfly, and before I could even answer, she'd left me there and fluttered off over the school yard to where Marie-Therese Schulze-Horn and Hubert Schulze-Eschenbach were standing.

I saw how they bent their heads close together and laughed, and I wished I could belong.

"What'd she want, then?" Daniel asked.

"Girl talk!" I answered, and ran to the schoolhouse.

"And don't stay out too late!" called my mother as I ran down the stairs. "Don't stay out too late! You got that?"

"Yeah, Mom!"

I pulled the door closed behind me and breathed a sigh of relief that she hadn't come out of the kitchen. I'd put on her absolute favorite yellow T-shirt, and she certainly would never have let me borrow it willingly. But I simply had to wear it today, for I wanted to look like Anna-Sofia.

Daniel and Lucas were bent over the parapet, the red-eye bucket at their feet.

"I see him!" Lucas cried excitedly and pointed at the green water. "There! There he goes! Boy, is he huge! C'mon, Daniel, let's haul him in!"

But Daniel shook his head.

"Not today! Tomorrow! The season starts tomorrow!"

"What's it matter!" groused Lucas. "One day sooner or later! The pike won't know the difference, will 'e! Why don'cha admit it. You're just too chicken!"

"Tomorrow!" said Daniel. "And not a day sooner!"

I climbed on my bike.

"Where you off to, then?" Lucas asked.

I pushed on the pedals and didn't answer.

Anywhere away from here, I thought, just away from here! For it seemed to me that beyond the grounds of the estate there was another land, a land without any pike, and without any tears, and without any oxygen tanks! And that's where I was going, where you could laugh loudly and giggle softly, where you petted kittens and gossiped about boys. That's where I was going and there, I would belong.

Anna-Sofia already stood in her butterfly-yellow dress before the ice-cream shop, waiting.

"Well, finally!" she said, and giggled as we walked inside. "I'll have the chocolate-hazelnut, and you?"

"Strawberry-vanilla!"

"Pronto, Signorine!" laughed the Italian ice-cream man. "Cioccolata-Nocciola e Fragola-Vanilla!"

That's what he did every time. He repeated our orders in Italian. Daniel and I always got a kick out of it, because it brought a piece of the great wide world into our little village. But Anna-Sofia rolled her eyes. "Stupid grease-ball!" she whispered to me. "He's been here forever and he still can't speak German properly!"

I wanted to defend the ice-cream man, but I didn't have the nerve and Anna-Sofia had already pulled me over to the corner booth and plopped herself down next to me on the green cushioned seat.

"But those greaseballs can sure make good ice cream!" she said.

I nodded.

She scooted closer to me.

"So do tell. What's the deal with Daniel's mother?"

"What d'you mean? What's there to tell?"

"Oh, you know! Everyone knows!"

I moved away from her. "Is that why you invited me out here?"

"Oh, don't be like that," said Anna-Sofia Schulze-Wettering. "I only wanted to know if it was true."

"If what's true?"

"If it's true that when Daniel's mother dies, his father's going to marry your mother!"

"Are you nuts?"

"But that's what everyone says!"

I sprung up.

"They've got a screw loose!"

Anna-Sofia pulled me back down in the seat.

"Now calm down! Didn't you know?"

I shook my head.

"Hmm, well, isn't that always how it is! The ones involved are always the last to find out!"

Anna-Sofia smiled. It was the kind of smile I'd seen on teachers when I'd given a very wrong answer. And it made me feel helpless and angry.

"And why would they say that?"

"Because your mother's always at Daniel's father's house. Until late at night. So, of course, people will talk!"

"But she's with Gisela! Daniel's father's not even there most of the time!"

Anna-Sofia raised her eyebrows.

"And why doesn't Gisela go to the hospital, then? That would make much more sense. She'd have everything she needs there! My mother says that it's real selfish to take advantage of people like that. And Daniel and Lucas shouldn't have to see all that misery, either, my mother says. That's what hospitals are for, aren't they!"

I was becoming more and more furious. Of course I'd already thought about it too. But in the hospital, they surely wouldn't have hung a mirror on the wardrobe. And if I myself had to chose between the hospital and my house, I'd rather lie in my own bed too.

Anna-Sofia chortled.

"Is it really true that Daniel's mother has to wear diapers now, like a baby? My mother told me that she has to be changed at least three times a day! That's gotta stink! If I were your mother, I'd simply gag!" She shuddered.

At that moment, something inside me snapped. Something squealed inside my head, like tires do when you suddenly slam on the brakes. My heartbeat pounded in my ears and everything came into sharp focus. I saw Anna-Sofia's glowing butterfly-yellow dress and her sneering grimace and those stupid freckles.

And my hand, with the ice-cream cone in it, raised up all by itself, and I held the ice-cream cone the wrong way 'round like a knife and smushed it in Anna-Sofia Schulze-Wettering's face, right between her blue kitten eyes. I heard the waffle cone crack and Anna-Sofia cry out, and the half-melted strawberry-vanilla mush slid down over her freckles and dripped onto the butterfly-yellow dress.

"You're gonna pay for that, you stupid cow!" Anna-Sofia screeched. "You're gonna pay for that!" Her voice cracked in outrage.

"Madonna mia!" cried the Italian ice-cream man.

But by then I was already on my bike, and pedaling as if I had the devil at my heels.

But instead of at my heels, the devil was suddenly standing right in front of me. He stood there as if he'd sprung up from the ground. I leaned into the brakes and nearly shot out over the handlebars.

And the devil looked just like our caretaker. With his heavy hunting boots and his green knee britches, hands planted on his hips, he glared at me in fish-eyed fury and began to bellow. What on earth did I think I was doing! This here was a park lane for walking, not a racetrack for teenyboppers!

I still remember perfectly that he said "teenyboppers," and I remember that I couldn't help grinning.

The caretaker sharply drew a breath.

"I'll be damned! And she smirks, to boot! Well, that just takes the cake!" he bellowed. "And no wonder, when the mother's got other plans and can't be bothered. You can tell your mother she'll be hearing from me! In writing!"

Great, him too, I thought.

"THERE ARE DAYS YOU FEEL LIKE you just can't get a leg up," my father would say. That was back when he used to tell me about the yahoos.

I remember that he took me on his lap and we looked out the window for a long time, and I asked: "Daddy, what are the yahoos, actually?"

And he'd sighed and said: "Those are very strange people who always copy everything they see!"

"Everything?" I'd asked.

"Everything, sweet pea!"

"And what if one of them stands on one leg?"

"Then all the other yahoos stand on one leg too!"

"And what if one falls over?"

"Then all the other yahoos fall over too!"

"And if one of them paints a picture?"

"Then all the other yahoos also paint a picture!"

"All of them, Daddy?"

"All of them!"

"But we're not yahoos, are we?"

"No, sweet pea!" my daddy said. "We are not yahoos!"

I had thought about the yahoos for weeks, had imagined where they might live, and what all they would copy, and what it would look like. I had thought it was all a fun game back then.

But that's because, back then, I didn't yet know that yahoos were actually real. Now the scales had fallen from my eyes. Anna-Sofia was a yahoo, and the caretaker, and Anna-Sofia's mother, and everyone who bad-mouthed my mother without having the slightest clue about anything.

"Everyone says your mother's going to marry Daniel's father!" Anna-Sofia had said.

Everyone. Those were the yahoos.

"You're home early!" said my mother. She sat with her feet up in the sun lounge by the millstone table in front of the house. "And? Was it nice?" I didn't answer, but I didn't go inside either. I just stood there and drew patterns in the dirt with my shoe. Actually, I was waiting for her to chew me out about the yellow T-shirt.

But she didn't. She just looked at me for a long time and then she said: "It suits you, that T-shirt! Do you want it?"

And then I burst into tears and she stood up and took me in her arms.

"It was that bad?" she asked.

"Worse!" I sobbed.

And then she held me tight and rocked me, and sang the "Cheer-up, cheer-up, goosey-goose" song like she used to.

Cheer-up, cheer-up, goosey-goose,
'twill all be right again.
The kitty's tail will not come loose,
'twill all be right again.
Cheer-up, cheer-up, mousey dear,
all's long gone this hundred year.

And then I told her everything. Everything that Anna-Sofia had said and what people were saying. And when I came to the part about how I shoved my ice-cream cone in Anna-Sofia's face, my mother burst out laughing and clapped her hands in glee. "Wonderful!" she cried. "And don't you worry about the caretaker! I can manage him!"

"And what about the other thing?" I asked. "About you and Peter?"

"Yahoo bullshit!" answered my mother.

———

THAT EVENING, I SAW GISELA for the last time.

My mother stood in the kitchen and spread liverwurst on our sandwiches.

"You can think about it some more," she said. "But Gisela asks about you often. You would really make her very happy!"

Daniel and Lucas sat on the kitchen bench and looked at me. I knew exactly what they were both thinking. I could see that they thought I was the biggest coward in the world. For the two of them had started going back into Gisela's sickroom. My mother told me that Lucas had even crawled into bed with her.

Yes, it was true what Daniel and Lucas thought. I was a coward. But I was terribly scared of seeing Gisela.

Outside, the doves were cooing.

And tomorrow was the first day of summer vacation.

And tomorrow, Daniel would catch the pike.

And if there really was a pike-god, then Gisela would get better anyway, and then I could go see her any old time . . . if there really was a pike-god!

My mother gave me a look.

"Quit biting your nails!"

Outside, the cries of the peacocks pierced the evening.

But if there were no pike-god, then maybe I'd have to carry around my guilty conscience forever. It would be just the way it was with my fear of German shepherds. That had stuck with me all this time, too, like a bad jinx, though my father had told me the secret of how to get rid of it. If there were no pike-god, then tonight might be my last opportunity to make Gisela happy. But I didn't know which way I should decide. After all, it was also a decision for or against the pike-god.

"Would you stop with the nail-biting already!" said my mother.

Startled, I took my finger out of my mouth.

"Your future's safe as houses!" whistled Daniel. Then he grinned.

If the peacock cries right now, I thought, then I'll go see Gisela. And just as I thought it, the caretaker's car came clattering over the drawbridge and the peacock screamed so loud that my ears hurt.

That evening, I saw Gisela for the last time.

She lay there, so small in the big, white bed, and she didn't look like Gisela at all. Not like the Gisela I knew. Her arms had gotten really thin and she couldn't open one hand. And the transparent oxygen mask covered her nose and slightly opened mouth, and sat tightly under her chin. Her eyes were different, too. They were much larger and darker, and as she looked at me, I had the feeling that her eyes were burning holes in my face.

I held my mother's hand tightly, but Mom broke free and shoved me forward to the edge of the bed. I saw that Gisela was smiling under the oxygen mask. With her healthy hand, she waved me on to come closer. I bent over her and then she took the mask off and whispered: "I'm so glad that you've come, my dear girl!"

I saw that her eyes glistened with tears, and I didn't know what I should say, so I said nothing. But Gisela simply pulled me toward her and gave me a kiss. And her arm on my shoulder was as light as a feather.

And then it was all over.

My mother helped Gisela put the mask back on and asked if she wanted some more pureed strawberries. But Gisela shook her head and Lucas threw himself on the bed from the other side and said: "Tomorrow we're going to catch the pike, Mommy! You'll see. He's sooooo big!"

Gisela rolled her eyes and shook her head again and Daniel stood stiffly at the foot of the bed, grinning sheepishly.

And meanwhile, the air from the oxygen tank hissed with Gisela's every breath, and it sounded a little like a steam engine pulling out of the train station.

"So!" said my mother to Daniel and Lucas. "Go on and tell your mom good night, now! And off you go to wash up, and don't forget to brush your teeth!"

She put her arm around me.

"And you go on back home! I'll come later!"

As I stood in the doorway and looked back, Gisela lifted her hand and waved to me, just like she used to from the office window, and, just like I used to, I waved back.

"GOOD LORD!" RAILED MY MOTHER. "A person goes to all that trouble to make some food, spends the whole morning at the stove, and all you guys can think about is fish!"

"Pike!" muttered Lucas.

"And right now's when they bite best!" said Daniel.

"And we can always eat our lunch later this evening! Please, Mom!"

My mother sighed and lit a cigarette and I ran to her and gave her a big hug.

"Now don't be so emotional all the time!" she laughed and broke free. "Well, go on then, get out of here!"

We ran headlong out of the kitchen.

"But you better bring my best knife back! You got that?"

And then all three of us were on the stone bridge, lying on our stomachs on the parapet and staring into the water. The sun pounded on our backs. A coot made its way jerkily under the bridge and Lucas threw bread crumbs. Daniel slowly let the trap down.

The water below us bubbled up. The redeye snapped greedily at the crumbs and Lucas cried: "Pull it up, man!"

The trap spun around quickly. Like a redeye merry-go-round. I was dizzy just looking at it.

Lucas tipped the bucket a bit and held it, and Daniel emptied the trap.

Then Daniel said: "That one there, in the middle, it looks pretty good!"

Lucas took the redeye out of the bucket. With his thumb and forefinger, he pushed its mouth open.

And while the redeye was looking like it was about to say "O," Lucas stuck the pike hook through its upper lip.

Daniel nudged me. "It didn't feel a thing!" he said. "They don't have any nerve endings!"

I knew that wasn't true, because it said in my fishing guide that fish are totally capable of feeling pain, and that fishing with live bait may be effective, but it was also cruel. That's exactly what it said, but I didn't say anything. I was just glad when Daniel threw the fishing line with the writhing redeye back in the water.

And then we waited and Daniel gave the line some slack and the redeye swam far out into the moat and we could see the trace of its wake and above us flew a heron and his reflection was black.

When the heron had gone, Daniel pulled on the line to test if the redeye was still wiggling. It flapped its tail and tried to dive back down.

"We're getting nowhere!" said Lucas. "If he doesn't bite now, he never will!"

Daniel gave the line more slack.

"Man, watch what you're doing!" cried Lucas. "It's swimming for the weeds!"

The shore was overgrown with small shrubs. And the old chestnut trees had bent their thick branches down, almost to the very surface of the water, as if they wanted to take a drink. The ivy that twined around them reached deep into the water. And that's just where the redeye was trying to flee.

And then everything happened very quickly.

For a tenth of a second, we saw the silver belly of the fish glisten under the water's surface. For a brief moment,

we caught a glimpse of how the great pike opened wide its maw, with its double row of teeth, and then we saw only circles in the water and the taut line sliding through Daniel's fingers. The pike dove under.

"We've got him!"

The spool of nylon cord danced in Daniel's hand as he let it roll itself out.

"Pull it up!" cried Lucas. "Pull it up already!"

But Daniel shook his head.

"He needs time! He has to swallow first! Otherwise he'll spit the hook back out again!"

"Should I get the net?" asked Lucas.

Daniel nodded.

Lucas climbed down the embankment with the net. Behind us, a car drove up into the courtyard. I saw that it was black, but we didn't pay it anymore attention.

"That's a good place!" Daniel called to Lucas. "I'll pull him over there!"

Lucas dipped the net under the water. He bit his lower lip and stared, spellbound, at the fishing line.

With a jerk, Daniel pulled it in.

The line stretched tight, as if it would break.

And then the pike came up.

He was much bigger than I had thought. Much bigger than the pictures in the fishing guide. And he fought and he whipped his tail around and tore and pulled at the line, but Daniel didn't let go. Foot by foot, he drew the pike toward the shore. And the pike reared itself up and for a moment I hoped the line would break, but then

Lucas stuck the net under the pike's belly, and the pike was inside.

He doubled up and bit the mesh. He tried to rip the net to shreds.

"Wow, we've got him!" cried Lucas. "We've really got him!"

Daniel ran down the embankment and both of them held the net and pulled it onto the bridge. The pike now lay very still, his powerful gills opening and closing. He had a huge mouth, and I saw his teeth. They were close together, hundreds of them, and all of them were sharp, like a cat's incisors.

The pike was beautiful. He shimmered a silvery green and he looked wild and dangerous. Even now, when he was half dead.

Daniel took a cudgel.

I turned away.

I didn't want to see how Daniel hit him. I didn't want to see him plunge the kitchen knife into the pike's head. I didn't want to see the pike heart beating in Daniel's hand.

I looked up. The sky above the red manor roof was deep and endlessly blue. The doves sat on the gutter. I saw our kitchen window. It was closed now. My mother stood behind the glass, smoking and crying.

I walked slowly toward the arched gate. In front of Gisela's door stood the doctor's car. The door was open.

I saw Peter come down the three steps to the yard. He held his head low. And he walked like an old man, real tired and slow. He walked right by me, quite close, but didn't see me.

And then I heard Lucas calling: "Daddy! We got him! Daddy, look at how big he is!"

And I turned around. And Peter was kneeling down and holding his boys in his arms. And the three had pressed their foreheads together and I saw Peter's back and his sobs.

I bent down over the parapet and stared into the water.

Two dragonflies whirred by; a coot dabbled for food and a school of little redeye sunned themselves just under the water's surface.

Everything was the same as always. It was as if nothing at all had happened.

Jutta Richter is among the most celebrated of authors of children's literature in Europe today. She has written more than twenty books, for which she has won several awards, including the German Youth Literature Award and the Herman Hesse Prize for her body of work. She lives in a castle in Munsterland, Germany, and also in Lucca, Tuscany.

Anna Brailovsky is the widely published translator of numerous academic and literary works, including Fyodor Dostoevsky's *The Idiot*. She lives in Minneapolis, Minnesota.

If you enjoyed this book, you'll also want
to read these other Milkweed novels.

Trudy by Jessica Anderson

*Milkweed Prize for
Children's Literature*

• Aging parents and a new
  school pose challenges for
  an eleven-year-old girl.

Runt by V. M. Caldwell

• A twelve-year-old boy forges
  an unusual friendship while
  dealing with the death of
  his mother.

Perfect by Natasha Friend

*Milkweed Prize for
Children's Literature*

• A thirteen-year-old girl
  struggles with bulimia
  after her father dies.

P*arents Wanted*
by George Harrar

*Milkweed Prize for
Children's Literature*

• Focuses on the adoption
  of a boy with ADD.

I Am Lavina Cumming
by Susan Lowell

*Mountains & Plains Booksellers
Association Award*

• This lively story culminates
  with the 1906 San Francisco
  earthquake.

A Bride for Anna's Papa
by Isabel R. Marvin

*Milkweed Prize for
Children's Literature*

• Life on Minnesota's Iron
  Range in the early 1900s.

Minnie by Annie M. G.
Schmidt

• A cat turns into a woman
  and helps a hapless news-
  paperman.

Behind the Bedroom Wall
by Laura E. Williams

*Milkweed Prize for
Children's Literature*

*Jane Addams Peace
Award Honor Book*

• Tells a story of the
  Holocaust through the
  eyes of a young girl.

**To order books or for more
information, contact Milkweed
at (800) 520-6455 or visit our
Web site (www.milkweed.org).**

MILKWEED ⬤ EDITIONS

Founded in 1979, Milkweed Editions is one of the largest independent, nonprofit literary publishers in the United States. Milkweed publishes with the intention of making a humane impact on society, in the belief that literature can transform the human heart and spirit. Within this mission, Milkweed publishes in four areas: fiction, nonfiction, poetry, and children's literature for middle-grade readers.

Join Us

Milkweed depends on the generosity of foundations and individuals like you, in addition to the sales of its books. In an increasingly consolidated and bottom-line-driven publishing world, your support allows us to select and publish books on the basis of their literary quality and the depth of their message. Please visit our Web site (www.milkweed.org) or contact us at (800) 520-6455 to learn more about our donor program.

Interior design and typesetting
by Percolator

Typeset in FF Celeste

Printed on HiBulk Natural paper
by Friesens Corporation